This book belongs to

BR100

For Rupert and Erin
(And with thanks to Peter Perspective)
C.F.

This book is printed on paper produced from
wood that comes from sustainably managed forests

First published in Great Britain in 2011 by
Gullane Children's Books
185 Fleet Street, London, EC4A 2HS
www.gullanebooks.com

This paperback edition first published in 2012

1 3 5 7 9 10 8 6 4 2

Text and illustrations © Charles Fuge 2011

The right of Charles Fuge to be identified as the author and illustrator of this work
has been asserted by him in accordance with the Copyright, Designs and Patents Act, 1988.
A CIP record for this title is available from the British Library.

ISBN:978-1-86233-867-8

Printed and bound in China

Charles Fuge's
Astonishing Animal
ABC

GULLANE
CHILDREN'S BOOKS

A, arty aardvark,
B, bouncing bear,

C, cosy cobra,
curled up in a
comfy chair.

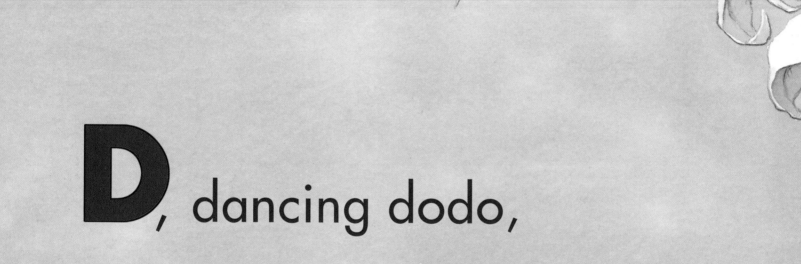

D, dancing dodo,

E, enormous egg,

F, fat flamingo,
feeling frightened,
on one leg.

G,
girl gorilla,

H and **I,**
hare on ice,

J, jolly jackal,
and his jelly-jumping mice.

K, king koala,

L, lion's lost,

M, mouse at market, asking, "What do mammoths cost?"

N, nasty narwhal,

O, outraged owl,

P, pirate penguin
and his panther,
on the prowl.

Q, quite quiet quail,

R, rhino row,

S, snoozy sloth needs sleep

and wants some silence **NOW!**

T, tortoise training

U, unicorn,

V, vulture visits vet (a Viking vole named Vaughn).

x-ray department ➡

W, worried walrus,

X and **Y**,
x-ray yak,

and **Z** is a zooming...

... ZUZZA ZOZZA ZIZZA
ZAK!

Other books by
Charles Fuge

Three Little Dinosaurs

My Dad!

This Is the Way

I Know a Rhino

Yip! Snap! Yap!

What Can a Baby Do?
WRITTEN BY Sarah Churchill

Blot and Og's Monster Party
WRITTEN BY Tasha Pym

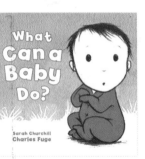

Little Wombat books

Sometimes I Like to Curl Up in a Ball
WRITTEN BY Vicki Churchill

Found You, Little Wombat!
WRITTEN BY Angela McAllister

Where to, Little Wombat?

Swim, Little Wombat, Swim!

Watch Out, Little Wombat!

The Adventures of Little Wombat
A collection of four fun-filled tales